The
WEREWOLF CLUB
#2

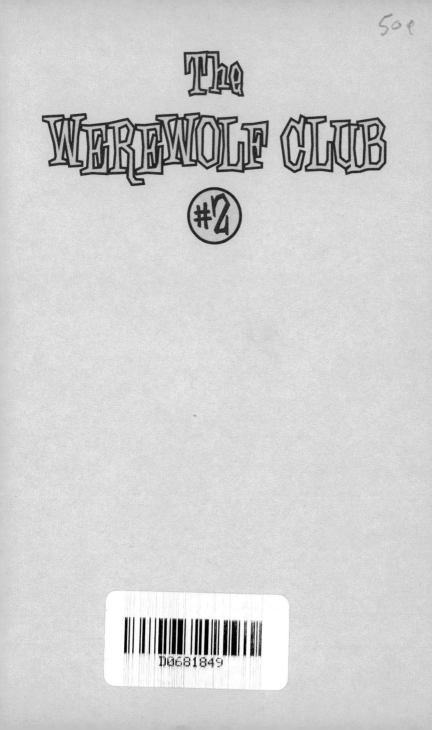

The
WEREWOLF CLUB

#2

The Lunchroom
of Doom

DANIEL PINKWATER

ALADDIN PAPERBACKS
New York London Toronto Sydney Singapore

First Aladdin Paperbacks edition September 2000

Copyright © 2000 by Daniel Pinkwater
Interior illustrations copyright © 2000 by Jill Pinkwater

Aladdin Paperbacks
An imprint of Simon & Schuster
Children's Publishing Division
1230 Avenue of the Americas
New York, NY 10020

Book design by Corinne Allen
The text for this book was set in Weidemann Book.
The illustrations were rendered in magic marker,
pen, and imported European wolf spit.

Printed and bound in the United States of America

10 9 8 7 6 5 4 3 2 1

Library of Congress Control Number: 00-107500

ISBN: 0-689-83845-X

CHAPTER ONE

WEREWOLF? WHERE?

After the werewolf ate the whole fourth-grade class, and their teacher, the people of the village of Fangdorf began to feel uneasy. There had been werewolves in the Black Forest for years and years, but never one as scary as this.

Old Hans, the woodsman, was good at hunting and tracking. He followed the footprints left by the werewolf.

"These paw prints will lead us to the werewolf's lair," Old Hans said. "Then we will catch it and make a werewolf stew with onions and potatoes. Yum."

The paw prints led not deep into the forest but back to the village. They led right up the main street, to the house of Old Hans's grandmother.

Through the window, Old Hans and the villagers saw the werewolf. At first they thought it had eaten the old lady, but then they saw it change into Old Hans's grandmother.

"My old granny is the werewolf?" Old Hans said. "Now I understand why she was always scratching."

The villagers ate the old lady with potatoes and onions, but it was a sad occasion, because they had always liked her.

And the werewolf of Fangdorf was never seen again.

CHAPTER TWO

WEE WEREWOLVES

"And that is the kind of story they used to tell about werewolves in the old country," Mr. Talbot said. "Is it any wonder people are afraid of us?"

"Imagine!" Lucy Fang said. "Eating a whole fourth-grade class. Who could believe such a thing?"

"It was sad when Old Hans ate his grandmother, even though everyone liked her," Ralf Alfa said.

"But it was cool when they looked through the window and saw her change from a wolf into a grandmother," I said.

"It was a great story! It made me hungry," Billy Furball said.

CHAPTER THREE

WE'RE HERE BECAUSE WE'RE WERE

We were sitting around the campfire in Mr. Talbot's backyard, toasting chunks of herring on long sticks. Mr. Talbot is the faculty adviser of the Watson Elementary School Werewolf Club. We have the only werewolf club in the whole school system.

My name is Norman Gnormal, by the way. My parents always wanted a dog—so that's how I was raised. I was well on the way to being somewhat weird when I became a werewolf. Now I fit in.

"Billy, what's this I hear about you having some problem in the lunchroom?" Mr. Talbot asked.

"I am banned from the lunchroom, possibly for life," Billy Furball said.

"Banned? What did you do?"

"I had a food fight . . . with myself," Billy Furball said.

"And they banned you?"

"It got to be a pretty big fight," Billy Furball said. "What's more, I have to see Dr. Cookie Mendoza, the Board of Education Psychiatrist."

"Wow! Cool!" we all said. "How big a food fight with yourself was it, anyhow?"

"They had to bring in special cleaning equipment overnight," Billy Furball said.

CHAPTER FOUR

WHEE! WEREWOLVES!

"If you are banned from the lunchroom, then none of us will eat in the lunchroom!" Ralf Alfa said.

"Ralf, that is a very nice thing to say," Mr. Talbot said. "I'm sure Billy appreciates it."

"I'm bringing bologna and banana sandwiches from home tomorrow. Six of them," Billy Furball said.

"And we, too, will bring lunch from home!" I said.

"But not bologna and banana sandwiches!" Lucy Fang said.

"My mom puts mayonnaise on them," Billy Furball said. "And sometimes a hard-boiled egg."

Knowing Billy Furball always makes me feel better about myself. No matter how abnormal I think I am, he's worlds ahead of me.

"So, it is decided! If our brother werewolf is not good enough to eat in the lunchroom—then neither are we! We will bring lunch from home, and share his exile!"

"It was only a matter of time until they would have thrown the rest of you out," Mr. Talbot said.

CHAPTER FIVE

WET WEREWOLVES

We ate our lunch with Billy Furball, sitting on the concrete curb next to the teachers' parking lot.

"Why isn't Mr. Talbot, our faculty adviser, with us?" Lucy Fang asked.

"He says since Billy Furball was not banned from the teachers' lunchroom it would be an empty gesture for him to stop eating there. Besides, this is vegetable soup day, and it's his favorite," Ralf Alfa explained.

"My mom put grape jelly on my bologna and banana sandwiches," Billy Furball said. "Anybody want to trade?"

"I see none of the regular kids joined in our

protest," I said. "They're all inside the lunchroom. Do you think that means they do not care about Billy Furball, a fellow Watson Elementary student, although a very strange one?"

"I think it means that they saw the rain clouds," Billy Furball said.

I looked up. "It does look like rain."

"It sure does," Lucy Fang said.

We felt the first fat drops. Big, wet spots appeared on our lunch bags. Then the drops fell faster. They went *splat* as they landed on our heads.

"This stinks," I said.

"Let's sing the werewolf song," Billy Furball said.

CHAPTER SIX

WEARY WEREWOLVES

For a while, we tried eating lunch in Mr. Talbot's car, but it smelled of diesel fuel, and it was full of shed-out fur. He hadn't vacuumed it in fifteen years.

"I'm tired of this!" Ralf Alfa shouted. "I want a hot lunch—even such a lunch as we get in the Watson Elementary School lunchroom! I'm tired of hanging out in Mr. Talbot's stinky car, and Billy Furball's bologna and banana sandwiches are giving me nightmares!"

We waited for Billy Furball to mention that his mother had made his bologna and banana sandwiches with sliced onions this particular day—which she had. Instead, he said, "Dr. Cookie Mendoza, the Board of Education Psychiatrist, says that nightmares are a key to the secrets of the human mind."

"Huh?" we all said.

CHAPTER SEVEN

WHERE THE WEREWOLVES
WENT

"Honest Tom's Tibetan-American Lunchroom!"

"What?"

"Honest Tom's Tibetan-American Lunchroom!" Lucy Fang repeated. "It's a neat place, and only a block from school."

"What's Tibetan-American?" I asked.

"No idea," Lucy Fang said. "The sign says, 'Try Our Oatmeal.' We can go there for lunch."

"Even Billy?"

"I had a look around," Lucy Fang said. "Compared with some of the regular customers, Billy Furball is like the Prince of Wales."

"Hey!" Billy Furball shouted. "Am not!"

"I just meant you were like some elegant

person, that's all," Lucy Fang said.

"I hate those royals," Billy Furball said.

Billy Furball is an antimonarchist.

CHAPTER EIGHT

WEREWOLVES ATE

Honest Tom's Tibetan-American Lunchroom had a big glass window, like a store window. Inside the window were a couple of dusty plants, some dead flies, and the sign that said, TRY OUR OATMEAL.

The floor was covered with red and black linoleum, and the walls were pale green. There were some tables, and a counter. Three big ceiling fans turned slowly. Pieces of paper, taped to the walls, flapped in the breeze from the fans. On the pieces of paper were written things like, SAUERKRAUT AND PEANUT BUTTER SANDWICH—75¢, and BORSCHT WITH TOAST—$1.

Behind the counter was Carla Lola Carolina. Carla Lola Carolina was the manager of Honest

Tom's Tibetan-American Lunchroom. It belonged to a guy named S. Alien. No one ever saw S. Alien. No one knew what the S. stood for. There was no Tom. Tom had sold the Tibetan-American Lunchroom years ago.

Carla Lola Carolina had a toothpick in her teeth and a rag in her hand. "What'll ya have, kiddos?" she asked the Watson Elementary Werewolf Club.

It was a real sophisticated place.

CHAPTER NINE

WEEPY WEREWOLVES

I forgot to mention that we Watson Elementary School werewolves were depressed and unhappy not only because we were sick of eating in Mr. Talbot's car. We were also deeply depressed because of the things Dr. Cookie Mendoza, Board of Education Psychiatrist, had been telling Billy Furball.

Dr. Cookie Mendoza, Board of Education Psychiatrist, claimed that Billy Furball was not a werewolf. She said that Billy couldn't be one— and none of us could be one, either—because . . . werewolves didn't exist! She had books to prove it. She said we might be hairy, we might drool, we might howl at the moon, we might feel like werewolves—but we could not be them . . .

because there was simply no such thing!

This made Billy Furball very sad indeed. Being a werewolf was the only thing he was good at. It made the other werewolves sad, too—the kids, that is. We never told Mr. Talbot what Dr. Cookie Mendoza, the Board of Education Psychiatrist, had said, because we were afraid it might push him over the edge, Mr. Talbot being of a delicate disposition.

It was with these thoughts in our minds that we first entered Honest Tom's Tibetan-American Lunchroom.

CHAPTER TEN

WE WOLF OUR FOOD

Honest Tom's Tibetan-American Lunchroom was a little more expensive than the lunchroom at school, but by sticking to the low end of the menu, we could afford to eat.

For our first meal we all chose the Tapioca Surprise. This was a bowl of tapioca pudding with whipped cream and a cherry on top. For the surprise, Carla Lola Carolina pushed with her finger a butterscotch candy into each portion of pudding. We selected grape soda as our beverage. It was an elegant lunch, and we felt rather grown up eating in a fine restaurant with our fellow citizens.

The others lunching at Honest Tom's Tibetan-American Lunchroom turned out to include some people we knew! Just as we had been seated at our table, Principal Pantaloni came in! He was walking arm-in-arm with Mr. Talbot! They nodded to us pleasantly, just as if we were some other adults they knew, and took seats at a table near the window.

The other lunchers included sailors, midgets, ladies with fancy clothes, a man in a turban, and another man with a big mustache and a brown leather jacket.

"You know who that is?" Carla Lola Carolina whispered to us when she brought our tapioca surprises. "That's Captain Sterling, of the North American Space Squad."

HOORAY FOR CAPTAIN STERLING

"I say," the man with the big mustache said, "might I borrow your bottle of Uncle Bob's Pennsylvania Hot Sauce?"

"Certainly, Captain Sterling," Lucy Fang said, handing him the bottle of Uncle Bob's. We noticed that he, too, had ordered the Tapioca Surprise.

"So, you know my name," Captain Sterling said while shaking hot sauce on his tapioca pudding.

"The lady at the counter told us," Billy Furball said.

"Carla Lola Carolina? Yes, she knows me," Captain Sterling said.

"She said you belong to the North American Space Squad," I said.

"This is true," said Captain Sterling. "I have been abducted by space aliens more than four hundred times."

"Wow!" we all said.

Captain Sterling leaned across his table and whispered, "The owner of this lunchroom is an alien—but he's one of the good ones."

"There are good and bad aliens?"

"Of course," Captain Sterling said. "On another subject, am I correct in observing that you children are all werewolves?"

CHAPTER TWELVE

WEREWOLVES WOW!

"Wow!" Ralf Alfa said. "Can you just tell that?"

"Neat!" I said.

"I'm impressed," Lucy Fang said.

"No. Not werewolves. No," Billy Furball said.

"No? Not?" we asked Billy Furball.

"No. Not. Not werewolves," Billy Furball said.

"How not?" we asked.

"Not because Dr. Cookie Mendoza, Board of Education Psychiatrist, explained it to me," Billy Furball said.

"She did?"

"She did," Billy Furball said. "She explained that we may think we are werewolves, we may feel like werewolves, we may act like werewolves, we may look like werewolves, we may even smell like werewolves . . . "

"That's what tipped me off," Captain Sterling said.

"But we are not werewolves. We only imagine ourselves to be werewolves. We can't be werewolves. Because . . . there is no such thing as a werewolf," Billy Furball finished sadly.

"Pish, tish, tosh, and shmootz," Captain Sterling said. "I know a werewolf when I smell one."

CHAPTER THIRTEEN

WOEFUL WEREWOLVES

"But Dr. Cookie Mendoza is a psychiatrist," Lucy Fang said. "And you . . . "

Carla Lola Carolina was standing near our table. "He's a man who lives in a room without a kitchen, and eats all his meals here."

"I have a telescope in my room," Captain Sterling said.

"That doesn't mean you know more than a psychiatrist," Carla Lola Carolina said.

"I've been abducted by space aliens," Captain Sterling said.

"Who hasn't?" Carla Lola Carolina said. "That doesn't make you an authority."

"You, too?" Captain Sterling asked Carla Lola

Carolina. "You've been kidnapped by aliens?"

"Oh, yes. They're always grabbing me, and taking me for rides in those darn spaceships," Carla Lola Carolina said.

"And do they threaten to turn you into a gigantic meatball if you talk?" Captain Sterling asked.

"Yes. And they also borrow my double-wide, four-slice toaster and keep it for weeks at a time. I hate those aliens. They're bad."

"But your boss isn't like that," Captain Sterling said.

"No. He's one of the good ones."

CHAPTER FOURTEEN

WEREWOLVES
WHIMPERING

"But what about us? Are we werewolves or not?" we asked.

"Well, Ms. Carla Lola Carolina is right," Captain Sterling said. "I'm no doctor—just a spaceman. If the psychiatrist says you can't be werewolves, I suppose you're probably not."

"But we like being werewolves. We're good at being werewolves. And you said yourself, we smell like werewolves."

"It's time to get back to school, kids," Mr. Talbot said. "Lunch period is almost over."

CHAPTER FIFTEEN

WHINING WEREWOLVES

"Did you hear what Billy Furball told us?" we asked Mr. Talbot. "He said that Dr. Cookie Mendoza, Board of Education Psychiatrist, says none of us can be werewolves because there is no such thing. Do you think that's true?"

"Listen, kids," Mr. Talbot said. "As a teacher, I am not allowed to get involved in anyone's mental health treatment. Besides, I have plenty of troubles of my own. My half brother, Lance Von Sweeny, is taking my mommy on a vacation to Transylvania, and if I want to go along, I have to pay for my own ticket, and my car has four bald tires, and I have a rash from wearing a flea collar . . . so I am not getting involved in this, okay?"

"But, Mr. Talbot, you're a werewolf yourself!"

"I'm not discussing this, so you can quit your whining."

Mr. Talbot is no good at coping with life, but he can be tough in his self-centered way. He wouldn't listen to another word on the subject.

CHAPTER SIXTEEN

WACKY WEREWOLF

The office of Dr. Cookie Mendoza, Board of Education Psychiatrist. Billy Furball is sitting in the big armchair, eating the hard candies.

BILLY FURBALL

So we can't possibly be werewolves?

DR. COOKIE MENDOZA

Not a chance. They're mythical.

BILLY FURBALL

So how do you explain us getting all hairy and toothy when there's a full moon?

DR. COOKIE MENDOZA

Group hysteria. You want to believe it, so it seems true.

BILLY FURBALL

Couldn't I have a blood test or something?

DR. COOKIE MENDOZA

There's no need, pal. You're not a werewolf, and your little friends aren't, either. It's just a game that got out of hand. You're confused, is all.

BILLY FURBALL

But we like being werewolves.

DR. COOKIE MENDOZA

I have no objection if you want to play that you're werewolves, as long as you understand you aren't, really. And I don't want you throwing gelatin desserts at yourself anymore.

BILLY FURBALL

That's a separate issue, arising from my dysfunctional family life.

DR. COOKIE MENDOZA

Time's up, buddy. I'll see you next week.

BILLY FURBALL

Your candy dish is almost empty. Do you ever have Tootsie Rolls in here?

DR. COOKIE MENDOZA

Nope. They make it hard to talk. Now, on your way, scamp.

CHAPTER SEVENTEEN

WASHED-UP WEREWOLVES

It was the night of the full moon. We gathered behind the Gas-for-Cheap gas station as usual. We silently filed into the woods behind the gas station. The moon came up.

We changed, the way we always did. Our noses and teeth got longer and longer, and turned into snouts and fangs. Our ears got long. Our arms and legs turned into long, strong paws . . . with claws. And we sprouted thick fur all over our bodies.

"It's not the same," Ralf Alfa said.

"No, it's not," Lucy Fang said. "Now that we know it's not real."

"It used to feel real. It still feels real, sort of," I said.

"Dr. Cookie Mendoza explained that," Billy Furball said. "It's a group hypnosis or something."

"I don't feel like running," I said.

"I don't, either," Ralf Alfa said.

"Let's go to the mall," Lucy Fang said.

CHAPTER EIGHTEEN

WANDERING WEREWOLVES

Four dejected werewolves scuffed along the upper and lower levels of the Grand Mall, sucking on grape snow cones and looking at the boring things in the stores.

Every now and then someone would notice us and scream, "Eeek! Werewolves!"

And we'd say, "Don't be stupid. There are no such things as werewolves. We're confused, is all."

After a few times back and forth, upper and lower, we decided to call it a night. We went home early.

41

CHAPTER NINETEEN

WONDERING
WEREWOLVES

The Watson Elementary School Imaginary Werewolf Club filed into Honest Tom's Tibetan-American Lunchroom.

This time, Carla Lola Carolina did not greet us with the exact words she had used since the second time we came there: "Hiya, kiddos. You want the usual?"

The usual was Tapioca Surprise all round, and grape sodas. It had become our favorite lunch, and we had picked up Captain Sterling's trick of shaking on a few drops of Uncle Bob's Pennsylvania Hot Sauce. But this time Carla Lola Carolina didn't seem to know that was what we always had.

"That's odd," Lucy Fang said when Carla Lola had served us our Tapioca Surprise.

"What's odd?" Ralf Alfa asked.

"Carla Lola Carolina usually pushes a butter-scotch candy into each tapioca pudding," Lucy Fang said. "That's the surprise. But this time she appears to have put in an olive."

"That is odd," Billy Furball said. "Good, though. And you know what else is odd?"

"What?" we asked.

"Well, I may have simply never noticed before, but don't you all think Carla Lola Carolina resembles a gigantic meatball?"

CHAPTER TWENTY

WARY WEREWOLVES

"You know, I thought she was a gigantic meat-ball, but I didn't want to say anything," I said.

"Was she always a meatball?" Ralf Alfa asked. "I am pretty sure she was a regular human yesterday."

Captain Sterling was sitting at the next table. "That is not Carla Lola Carolina," he whispered.

"Not?" we whispered back.

"Not," he whispered in an even lower whisper.

"Then what, or who?" we whispered.

"It is a life-form from another planet," Captain Sterling whispered so low, we could barely hear him. "And, it is not one of the good ones."

CHAPTER TWENTY-ONE

WORRIED WEREWOLVES

"Did Carla Lola Carolina change into that meatball from another planet?" we asked Captain Sterling.

"I'd say it took her place," Captain Sterling whispered.

"Took her place? Then where's Carla Lola Carolina?"

"Just don't get the meatball mad at you," Captain Sterling whispered. "Leave her a nice tip."

Then, Captain Sterling, of the North American Space Squad, paid his bill, left a nice tip, and hurried out of Honest Tom's Tibetan-American Lunchroom.

CHAPTER TWENTY-TWO

WEREWOLF WARNING

"Mr. Talbot! Carla Lola Carolina has turned into an enormous meatball! She's a life-form from another planet, and not one of the good ones! What shall we do?" We crowded around his desk when we got back to school.

"It is very bad manners to refer to anyone as an enormous meatball," Mr. Talbot said. "And children should not point out little defects in adults. Ms. Carla Lola Carolina is not an attractive woman, but she is a good person."

"It isn't her! The alien being has replaced her! We don't even know what happened to the real Carla Lola Carolina! Captain Sterling explained it to us."

"Captain Sterling is entitled to his opinion. But,

47

just think about this: What if Carla Lola Carolina is just having a bad-face day, or forgot to put on make-up, or woke up looking like a meatball for no known reason? Wouldn't it be cruel to get all excited and accuse her of being a space alien?" Mr. Talbot lectured us, wagging his finger.

"Well, what should we do?"

"Do nothing," Mr. Talbot said. "Behave normally, and behave politely, and be a credit to Watson Elementary School, and to the Werewolf Club."

CHAPTER TWENTY-THREE

WOBBLY-KNEED WEREWOLVES

It was Billy Furball's day to see Dr. Cookie Mendoza, Board of Education Psychiatrist, so it was only three members of the Watson Elementary Werewolf Club who went to Honest Tom's Tibetan-American Lunchroom: Ralf Alfa, Lucy Fang, and me, Norman Gnormal.

There was Carla Lola Carolina—she was still a meatball. There was Mr. Talbot, eating pancakes with Principal Pantaloni. There were the usual sailors, and acrobats, and ladies, and Vikings, eating their lunch. And there was Captain Sterling! He had turned into a meatball!

"It is worse than we thought," Lucy Fang said.

"Yes," Ralf Alfa said. "It appears to be creeping

meatballism! Who knows which of us will be next!"

It was a chilling thought.

Captain Sterling—or the meatball Captain Sterling—smiled and nodded to us, but he didn't say anything.

"It's an invasion, you know," I said. "If we were real werewolves, we could save the planet."

"But we're not," Ralf Alfa said.

"But we are!" Billy Furball said.

"Billy Furball!" we said. "What are you doing here? Weren't you supposed to be visiting your psychiatrist?"

CHAPTER TWENTY-FOUR

WELL DONE, WEREWOLF!

"I went to the office of Dr. Cookie Mendoza, Board of Education Psychiatrist," Billy Furball said. "And I found that she had become an enormous meatball. I asked her what this meant, and she told me she was part of a vast plan to invade our planet. She said that humans (and werewolves) would soon be no more—replaced with other-worldly meatballs."

"What did you say to that?" we asked Billy Furball.

"There was nothing to say," Billy Furball said. "What could I say? I ate her."

"You ate your psychiatrist?" We were astounded. "That doesn't sound like something a normal person could do."

"Well, I was able to," Billy Furball said.

"Because . . . "

"Because you're a werewolf!" we shouted.

We looked at each other. Then we looked at the meatball that had replaced Carla Lola Carolina, and the meatball Captain Sterling.

"Save the earth! Save the earth!" we shouted.

CHAPTER TWENTY-FIVE

WIPED-OUT WEREWOLVES

NOTE FROM THE EDITOR: This chapter contains things too ghastly and horrible for the eyes and minds of children, so it has been eliminated, and we offer instead the nice picture below:

CHAPTER TWENTY-SIX

WEREWOLF WICTORY

Soon it was all over. We found the real Carla Lola Carolina and Captain Sterling tied up in the vegetable bin in the kitchen of Honest Tom's Tibetan-American Lunchroom. They smelled of onions, but were otherwise all right.

As far as anyone knows, there have been no more instances of gigantic meatballs replacing citizens of Earth.

The real Dr. Cookie Mendoza was never found.

Mr. Talbot was proud of us for saving Earth, and Principal Pantaloni reinstated Billy Furball's school lunchroom privileges.

The Watson Elementary School Werewolf Club left the scene of our heroic struggle against evil

beings from another planet and went for a walk in the woods behind the gas station.

"How do you feel?" we asked one another.

"I feel . . . full," I said.

"I, too, feel full," Lucy Fang said.

"And I . . . I feel full also," Ralf Alfa said.

"I feel that I have absorbed a lot of insight and self-knowledge," Billy Furball said.

End